ISLANDBORN

ISLANDBORN

by Junot Díaz   illustrated by Leo Espinosa

Dial Books
for Young
Readers

Every kid in Lola's school was from somewhere else.
Hers was the school of faraway places.
Mai was from a city so big that it was like its own country.
India and Camila were from a stony village at the tippy top of the world.
Matteo had lived in a desert so hot even the cactus fainted.
Nu was born in a jungle famous for its tigers and its poets.

And Lola was from the Island.

So when her teacher, Ms. Obi, told the class, "Please draw a picture of the country you are originally from, your first country, and bring it in tomorrow," everyone got super excited.

"I'm going to put in pyramids," said Dalia.

"And I'll draw a canal *this* long," Franklyn said.

"There's gonna be a mongoose in mine," Nelson yelled. (Nelson always yelled.)

Everyone was talking about their drawings . . . everyone but Lola.

Lola, you see, loved to draw, but she had left the Island when she was just a baby so she didn't remember any of it.

Lola raised her hand. (She hated raising her hand almost as much as she hated Nelson's yelling.) "Miss, what if you don't remember where you are from? What if you left *before* you could start remembering?"

"No problema," Ms. Obi said. "Are there people around you who do remember?"

"Like my whole neighborhood!" Lola said. "And they're *always* talking about the Island."

"Well, then," Ms. Obi started, "maybe—"

But Lola finished her sentence. "I should talk to everyone who *does* remember. I should draw from their memories."

"That's a very good plan, Lola," Ms. Obi said with a smile.

Lola started feeling better about the assignment. But then she saw all the other kids chatting excitedly about what they were going to draw, and it made her sad. Everybody was remembering their first home, even Nelson who forgot everything. (Nelson even forgot his last name once, for like an hour.) Lola had always wanted to remember the Island, but no matter how hard she tried she never could. It was like a familiar word just at the tip of your tongue, but instead of a word this was an entire world! Lola closed her eyes and tried to recall *anything* about the Island but nothing came up.

She kept trying all through the school day—to help her focus,
she put her fingers on the sides of her head, like her abuela's
psychic sometimes did.

"Are you okay?" her cousin Leticia asked as they walked home from school together.

"I have to draw a picture of the Island," Lola explained, "but I was just a baby when we left! Prima, you have to help me."

"I don't remember a lot either, except for the bats. They were as big as blankets, and they used to chase after me at night."

"Blanket bats!" Lola pulled out her notebook and began to sketch.

Leticia stopped Mrs. Bernard who always sold them crispy empanadas after school. "Mrs. Bernard, what do you remember most about the Island?"

"Why, the music, of course! The whole country is like the inside of a güira. Like the inside of a drum."

"You mean like our neighborhood?" Lola said. The neighborhood had so much music it was like a radio with the dial broken off.

"On the Island there's even more music! There's more music than air! And everyone is always dancing. Even in their sleep people dance."

"Sleep dancing!" Lola sketched.

MERENGUE
BACHATA

Leticia led Lola into the barbershop that her brother Jhonathan owned. "Lola has to do an assignment about the Island. She needs to know what you remember most about it."

"Wepa," said Jhonathan, laughing. "The agua de coco. How wonderful it tastes when you drink it right from the coconut."

Mr. Rodriguez sat up in the chair. "And the mangoes that are the size of your head and so sweet—"

"They make you want to cry?" Lola said. (She loved mangoes.)

"That's it exactly!"

"How much color there is," said the woman waiting with her son. "Colorful cars, colorful houses, flowers everywhere. Even the people are like a rainbow—every shade ever made."

"Like us in here?" Lola said.

"Even more color," the woman said.

"Agua, mango heads, rainbow people." Lola was trying to keep up. "The Island sounds so beautiful. Why did we even leave?"

"Well, it isn't all beautiful," the woman's son said. "The heat is on you like five bullies."

The oldest barber muttered, "And other things."

Like what? Lola wanted to ask, but the oldest barber had already turned away.

In the lobby of their building the cousins ran into Mr. Mir, the superintendent. Leticia called out, "Hey, Mr. Mir, can you tell us what you most remember about the Island?"

"Nobody cares about that old stuff," Mr. Mir grumbled. "Just be glad that you live here."

"Don't listen to him," Leticia said. "Keep going and call me later if you need any help. Okay?"

"I will," Lola said.

When Lola got into the elevator she put her fingers on her temples and closed her eyes. "Island," she called, like it was a cat.

"Island!"

But like a cat, the Island did not come.

At home Lola found her abuela at the kitchen table trying to finish a puzzle. (Abuela loved puzzles.)

"Abuela! I'm supposed to draw a picture of the Island for school. But I don't remember it—*why* don't I remember it?"

"Hija, you were just a baby when you left."

"But the other kids remember . . . "

"Just because you don't remember a place doesn't mean it's not in you."

"Will you tell me what *you* remember most?" Lola asked.

"Of course! What I remember most is . . . the beaches. Hija, our beaches are poetry . . . you know when you hear your favorite poem? That's how it is to be on our beaches. Fish jump from the waves into your lap, and at sunset sometimes the dolphins will come out of the water to bow good night. And up north, where I'm from, there are even whales in the surf."

"Beach poetry! Dolphins! Surfing whales!" Lola sketched as fast as she could.

Lola's mother stuck her head in from the kitchen. "Hija, what *I* remember most is the hurricane that hit the Island right after you were born. Like the biggest baddest wolf of all! It huffed and puffed and blew thousands of houses into the sky!"

"Where were we?" Lola asked, her eyes wide.

"We were hiding under the bed is where we were!" Abuela said.

"That's right," her mother said. "And you know what? You never cried once. You were such a brave little girl."

"I wish I could remember *that*." Lola sighed.

"Well, it happened," her mother said. "You might not remember the Island but it remembers you."

"You should really talk to Mr. Mir," Abuela suggested. "He knows more about the Island than almost anybody."

"We tried asking him," Lola said, "but he didn't want to help."

"Mr. Mir can be a little grouchy sometimes. Let me talk to Mrs. Mir. I bet you we can get him to help."

Abuela called downstairs and shouted at Mrs. Mir, who then shouted at Mr. Mir. The old people were always shouting at each other; that's how they talked. (Maybe Nelson was an old person in training.)

"Go on down," Abuela said. "Mr. Mir said he would try to help."

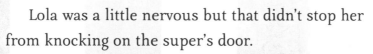

Lola was a little nervous but that didn't stop her
from knocking on the super's door.

Mrs. Mir let her in. "Look how big you've gotten,
Lola! Mr. Mir is in his workshop. Go right on in."

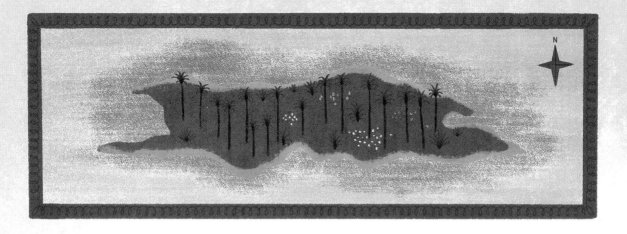

Mr. Mir looked up from the contraption he was fixing. "Your grandma says you've been interviewing people about the Island."

Lola nodded nervously. "Yes, sir. It's for a class assignment."

"What have they told you?"

She flipped through her sketches. "Bat blankets, more music than air, fruit that makes you cry, beach poems, and a hurricane like a wolf."

"I see," Mr. Mir said. "So no one told you about the Monster?"

Lola's eyes got wide. She shook her head *no*.

"Even those who know don't always want to talk about HIM."

Mr. Mir turned toward the old worn map he had of the Island. "Our Island has always been a beautiful place. It was when I was your age, and it is today. But even the most beautiful places can attract a monster. A long time ago, long before you were born, that's exactly what happened: A monster fell upon our poor Island."

For once Lola's pencil didn't move.

"It was the most dreadful monster anyone had ever seen. The whole Island was terrified and no one could defeat it. It was just too strong. For thirty years the Monster did as it pleased. It could destroy an entire town with a single word and make a whole family disappear simply by looking at it."

Lola's curly hair was uncurling with fear. "Did *you* see the Monster, Mr. Mir?"

"Yes. All the time."

"Were you scared?"

"We were all very scared."

Lola's heart was pounding. "So what happened next, Mr. Mir?"

"What should always happen to monsters. Heroes rose up. Strong smart young women just like you, Lola, and a few strong smart young men, too. They got tired of being afraid and fought the Monster. What a titanic battle that was. The whole Island shook from their struggle—the Monster tried all of its evil tricks but in the end the heroes found the Monster's weakness and banished it forever."

"Wao," Lola whispered. "What happened to the heroes?"

"No one knows, really. It was so long ago." Mr. Mir took off his glasses and sighed. "Anyway you should get back upstairs. It's getting close to dinnertime."

"Thank you, Mr. Mir," Lola said. "Thank you for all your help."

"How did it go?" Lola's mother asked.

"It was really good." Lola looked at the blank page in her hands.

Lola spent the rest of the night drawing the Island. She started out with one page, but she needed more room, so she added another page and then another and soon she had a book! She worked through dinner, and she worked in bed, and was just finishing the last touches on the cover when her abuela came in to check on her.

Abuela picked up a drawing of the final battle. And she got really still.

"Abuela, did you know about the Monster?"

"Of course, hija. Why do you think so many of us are here in the North?"

Lola put her arms around her abuela. "You must have been so scared!"

"Sometimes we were," her abuela whispered. "But we were also brave."

The next day it snowed. Lola put on her scarf and boots and stuffed her assignment under her coat. "Bendición, Mami! Bendición, Abuela!"

"Bendición, hija," they both called. "Good luck!"

Mr. Mir was pushing garbage cans against the curb. "Thank you, Mr. Mir, slayer of monsters!"

He laughed. "Good luck, Lola, daughter of heroes."

In class all the students were buzzing about their pictures. Nelson's mother had baked cupcakes for everyone so it was like a little party. Ms. Obi hung the drawings on the wall. "Now our classroom has windows," she said. "Anytime you want to look at one another's first homes all you have to do is look out the windows."

Then Ms. Obi reached Lola's desk. "So how did it go, Lola? Were you able to remember anything?"

"I tried really really hard but nothing came and that made me feel bad. But then I realized that I don't have to feel bad because even if I'd never set foot on the Island it doesn't matter: The Island is me."

Nelson snorted. "That is so *corny*."

"It is not!"

"Nelson, be nice," Ms. Obi said.

She and the other students gathered around Lola's desk. (Nelson made sure he got real close so he could see everything.) Lola suddenly got nervous.

"Go ahead, Lola, show us."

"Okay," Lola said. Taking a deep breath, she opened her book—

—and out burst the Island.

To Camila, Dalia, Matteo, India, and Mai—sorry it's late.
To Leo—for your brilliance.
To my querida Marjorie—for the love that brought this book to life.
And finally to the Island—for everything.
—J.D.

To Laura and Colombia, my Islands
—L.E.

....

Dial Books for Young Readers
Penguin Young Readers Group
An imprint of Penguin Random House LLC
375 Hudson Street, New York, NY 10014

Text copyright © 2018 by Junot Díaz. Illustrations copyright © 2018 by Leo Espinosa.

Library of Congress Cataloging-in-Publication Data

Names: Díaz, Junot, 1968– author. | Espinosa, Leo, illustrator.
Title: Islandborn / Junot Díaz ; illustrated by Leo Espinosa.
Description: New York, NY : Dial Books for Young Readers, 2018. | Summary:
"Lola was just a baby when her family left the Island, so when she has to
draw it for a school assignment, she asks her family, friends, and
neighbors about their memories of her homeland . . . and in the process, comes
up with a new way of understanding her own heritage" —Provided by publisher.
Identifiers: LCCN 2017006468 | ISBN 9780735229860 (hardcover)
Subjects: | CYAC: Islands—Fiction. | Dominican Americans—Fiction.
Schools—Fiction. | Immigrants—Fiction. | Dominican Republic—
History—1930–1961—Fiction. | Africa—Emigration and immigration—Fiction.
Classification: LCC PZ7.1.D4988 Isl 2018 | DDC [E]—dc23
LC record available at https://lccn.loc.gov/2017006468

Printed in U.S.A.
2 4 6 8 10 9 7 5 3

Design by Jasmin Rubero • Text set in Fiesole Text

The artwork for Islandborn was created digitally with Photoshop and mixed media.